ERIC CARLE

The Tiny Seed

READY-TO-READ

SIMON SPOTLIGHT

New York   London   Toronto   Sydney   New Delhi

This book was previously published with slightly different text.

SIMON SPOTLIGHT

An imprint of Simon & Schuster Children's Publishing Division

1230 Avenue of the Americas, New York, New York 10020

Copyright © 1987 Eric Carle Corporation

Eric Carle's name and signature logo type are registered trademarks of Eric Carle.

First Simon Spotlight Ready-to-Read edition May 2015

SIMON SPOTLIGHT, READY-TO-READ, and colophon are registered trademarks of Simon & Schuster, Inc.

For information about special discounts for bulk purchases, please contact Simon & Schuster Special Sales
at 1-866-506-1949 or business@simonandschuster.com.

The Simon & Schuster Speakers Bureau can bring authors to your live event. For more information or to book
an event contact the Simon & Schuster Speakers Bureau at 1-866-248-3049 or visit our website at
www.simonspeakers.com.

Manufactured in the United States of America 0315 LAK

10 9 8 7 6 5 4 3 2 1

Cataloging-in-Publication Data is available from the Library of Congress.

ISBN 978-1-4814-3576-5 (hc)

ISBN 978-1-4814-3575-8 (pbk)

This book was previously published with slightly different text.

It is Autumn.
A strong wind is blowing.
It blows flower seeds high in the air
and carries them far across the land.

One of the seeds is tiny.
It is smaller than any of the others.
Will it be able to keep up
with the others?
And where are they all going?

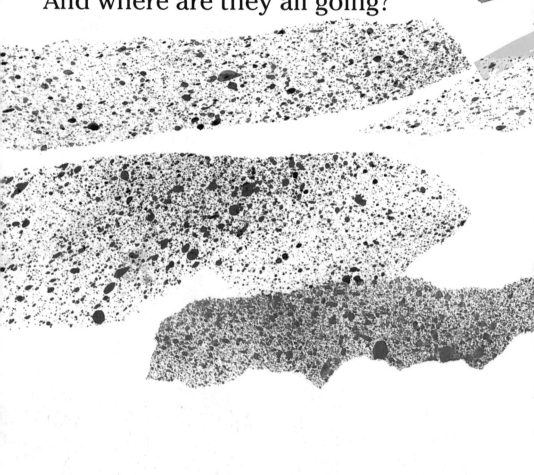

One of the seeds flies
higher than the others.
Up, up it goes! It flies too high and
the sun's hot rays burn it.
But the tiny seed sails
on with the others.

Another seed lands on a
tall and icy mountain.
The ice never melts,
and the seed cannot grow.
The rest of the seeds fly on.
But the tiny seed does not go
as fast as the others.

Now they fly over the ocean.
One seed falls into the water.
The others sail on with the wind.
But the tiny seed does not go as
high as the others.

One seed drifts down onto the desert.
It is hot and dry,
and the seed cannot grow.
Now the tiny seed is flying very low,
but the wind pushes it on
with the others.

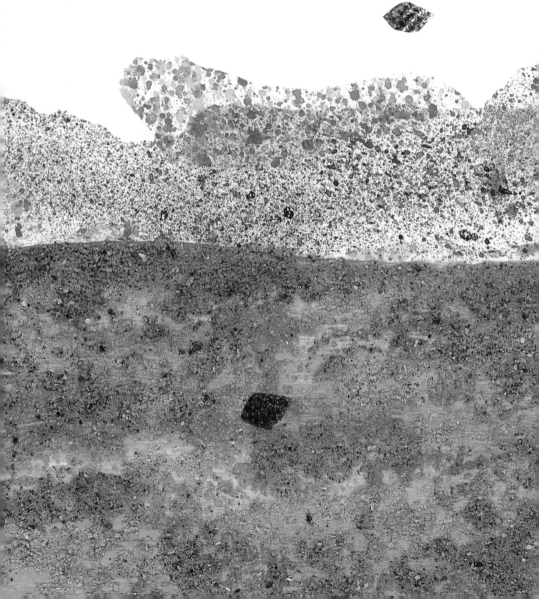

Finally the wind stops and the seeds
fall gently down on the ground.
A bird comes by and eats one seed.
The tiny seed is not eaten.
It is so small that the bird does not
see it.

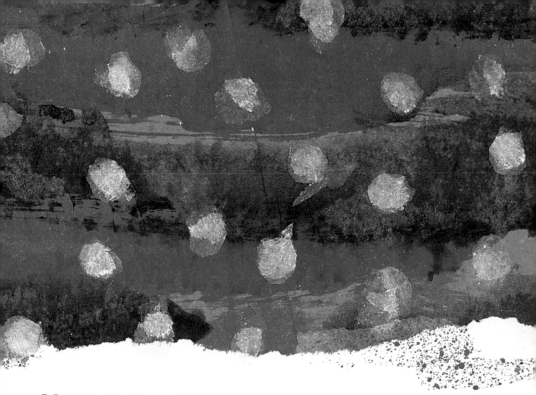

Now it is Winter.
After their long trip the seeds
settle down.
They look as if they are going to sleep
in the earth.
Snow falls and covers them like a
soft white blanket.

A hungry mouse that lives in the
ground eats a seed for his lunch.
But the tiny seed lies very still
and the mouse does not see it.

Now it is Spring. After a few months the
snow has melted.
Birds fly by. The sun shines. Rain falls.
The seeds grow so round and full
they start to burst open.
Now they are plants.

First they send roots down into the
earth.
Then their stems and leaves
begin to grow up toward the sun.
There is another plant that grows
much faster than the new little plants.
It is a big fat weed.

And it takes all the sunlight and the rain away from one of the small new plants.

The tiny seed has not begun to grow yet.
It will be too late! Hurry!
But finally it too starts to grow
into a plant.

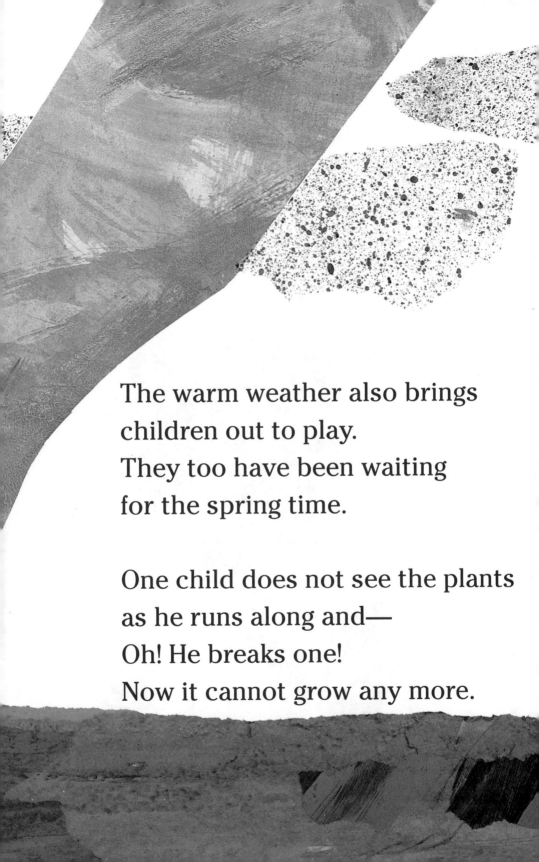

The warm weather also brings
children out to play.
They too have been waiting
for the spring time.

One child does not see the plants
as he runs along and—
Oh! He breaks one!
Now it cannot grow any more.

The tiny plant that grew from the tiny
seed is growing fast, but its neighbor
grows even faster.
Before the tiny plant has three leaves
the other plant has seven!
And look! A bud!
And now even a flower!

But what is happening?
First there are footsteps,
then a shadow. Then a hand reaches
down and breaks off the flower.

A boy has picked the flower
to give to a friend.

It is Summer.
Now the tiny plant from the tiny seed
is all alone.
It grows on and on.
The sun shines on it
and the rain waters it.
It has many leaves.
It grows taller and taller.
It is taller than the people.
It is taller than the trees.
It is taller than the houses.

And now a flower grows on it.
People come from far and near
to look at this flower.
It is the tallest flower they have
ever seen.

All summer long the birds and
bees and butterflies come visiting.

They have never seen such a
big and beautiful flower.

Now it is Autumn again.
The days grow shorter.
The nights grow cooler.

The wind carries yellow and red
leaves past the flower.
Some petals drop from the giant flower.
They sail along with the bright leaves
over the land and down to the ground.

The wind blows harder.
The flower has lost almost all
of its petals.
It sways and bends away from the wind.
But the wind grows stronger and
shakes the flower.

Once more the wind shakes the flower, and this time the flower's seed pod opens.

Out come many tiny seeds that quickly sail far away on the wind.